MANCROW'S FEATHER

First-Start® Legends

MANCROW'S FEATHER

A STORY FROM JAMAICA

Retold by Janet Palazzo-Craig
Illustrated by Philip Kuznicki

Troll

Long ago, a girl named Solidae lived with her grandmother. Solidae was strong and clever. Each day, she climbed trees to pick coconuts. And each day, she caught colorful fish in her net.

One morning, Solidae saw something strange. The many-colored fish she usually caught were now the color of mud. "What has happened, Grandmother?" she asked.

"Mancrow is back," said her grandmother. "He is a creature half-bird, half-man—and a troublemaker!"

Then she said, "Mancrow once had colorful feathers. When it was time for him to become either a man or a bird, he refused. He hid in the dark forest, and all but one of his colorful feathers turned black.

"Solidae, I must go to the village for a few days. Promise me you will not speak to Mancrow."

Solidae promised. Then off she went to pick mangoes.

She soon saw her colorful friend Iguana in a tree. She climbed up after him. Playfully, he ran away. But he slipped and fell to the ground.

Suddenly, an angry voice called, "Who are you, clumsy creature? I will punish you."

Solidae saw a beast—half-man, half-bird—standing over Iguana. Mancrow! "Do not hurt my friend!" she said, forgetting her promise.

"Who said that?" asked Mancrow, turning. As he did, Iguana ran away.

When Solidae saw Iguana, she could not believe her eyes. His beautiful colors were gone! "Mancrow, you did this," she said. "Give Iguana back his colors!"

"Nonsense," said Mancrow. "Look at me, girl, and you will see beauty."

"Do not look," warned Iguana. "When I did, I could not move."

Solidae was careful not to look at Mancrow. "Go!" she shouted.

"I will go," said Mancrow. "But you will not forget me!"

He spread his black wings. The sky grew dark. "Now all color is mine," he said. Then Mancrow was gone.

Solidae and Iguana walked home in the dark. "This is my fault," said Solidae.

"Not so," said Iguana. But still Solidae felt very sad.

Days passed. Daylight did not come. Solidae saw the leaves falling from the trees. The forest was dying without light to give it life.

Finally, her grandmother came home. Solidae told her what had happened. "Where did the colors go?" Solidae asked.

"Mancrow keeps them in his one colorful feather. If he were to lose that feather, his power would end."

Solidae made up her mind. "I will pluck that feather," she said.

She packed cakes to eat and her fishing net. Then she set off for the forest.

When she reached the forest, Solidae climbed a tree. She put the cakes out on a branch. Then she sang a song, calling Mancrow to join her.

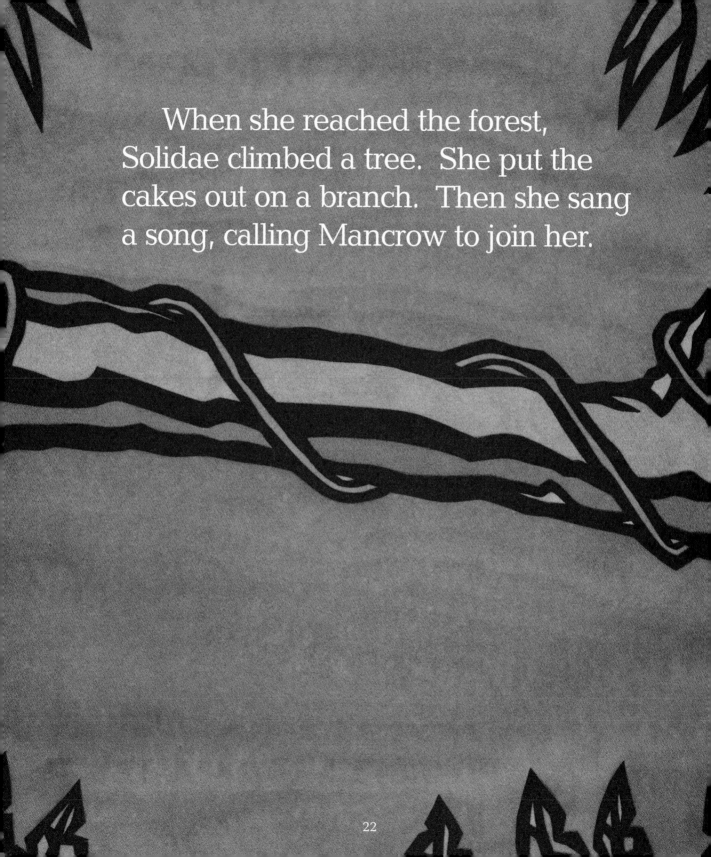

Soon she heard his black wings beating nearby.

"I have come to praise you," said Solidae.

Mancrow spread his wings proudly. "See how beautiful I am?" he said.

"Come closer," said Solidae. "Eat some cake."

As Mancrow tried to land on the branch, he slipped. Solidae quickly took her net and caught him!

Mancrow turned and twisted, ripping the net with his claws.

Solidae jumped on the net, trying to find Mancrow's one colorful feather. "Help!" she called.

All the forest creatures came.
They held Mancrow down.
Solidae found the
feather and plucked it!

As Solidae held the feather up, morning light filled the sky. The people and animals danced with joy. Mancrow ran off to hide.

Time has passed, but Solidae has not forgotten Mancrow. When dark storms come, she still watches closely to make sure he has not returned. If he does, brave Solidae will be ready for him!

The Caribbean Islands

Florida

Jamaica

Mancrow's Feather is a legend from the Caribbean island of Jamaica. It is a tale that is thought to have been brought to Jamaica long ago by slaves from West Africa. Today, Jamaica's population includes people of many races. Its national motto is "Out of Many, One People."